The Bear in the Cave

By Michael Rosen   Illustrated by Adrian Reynolds

BLOOMSBURY
CHILDREN'S
BOOKS

I'm a bear in a cave.
In a cave?
In a cave.
All alone.

I'm a bear all alone.
All alone?
All alone.

For Elsie and Emile – M.R.

For Rebecca – A.R.

First published in Great Britain in 2007 by Bloomsbury Publishing Plc
36 Soho Square, London, W1D 3QY

Text copyright © 2007 Michael Rosen
Illustrations copyright © 2007 Adrian Reynolds

The moral rights of the author and illustrator have been asserted

Audio CD produced by Jeff Capel at The Audio Workshop
Read by Michael Rosen

Copyright in recording © and ℗ Bloomsbury Publishing Plc 2007

A CIP catalogue record of this book is available from the British Library

ISBN 978 0 7475 7765 2

Printed and bound in China

1 3 5 7 9 10 8 6 4 2

And I sing to myself all day.
Do bee doo
Do bee doo
Do bee doodily doo.

I walk by the sea.
By the sea?
By the sea.

And I play with the waves all day.
    Splishety splash
        Splishety splash
            Splishety splashety splish.

One day I heard a noise.
Heard a noise?
Heard a noise.

It came from far away.
Far away?
Far away.

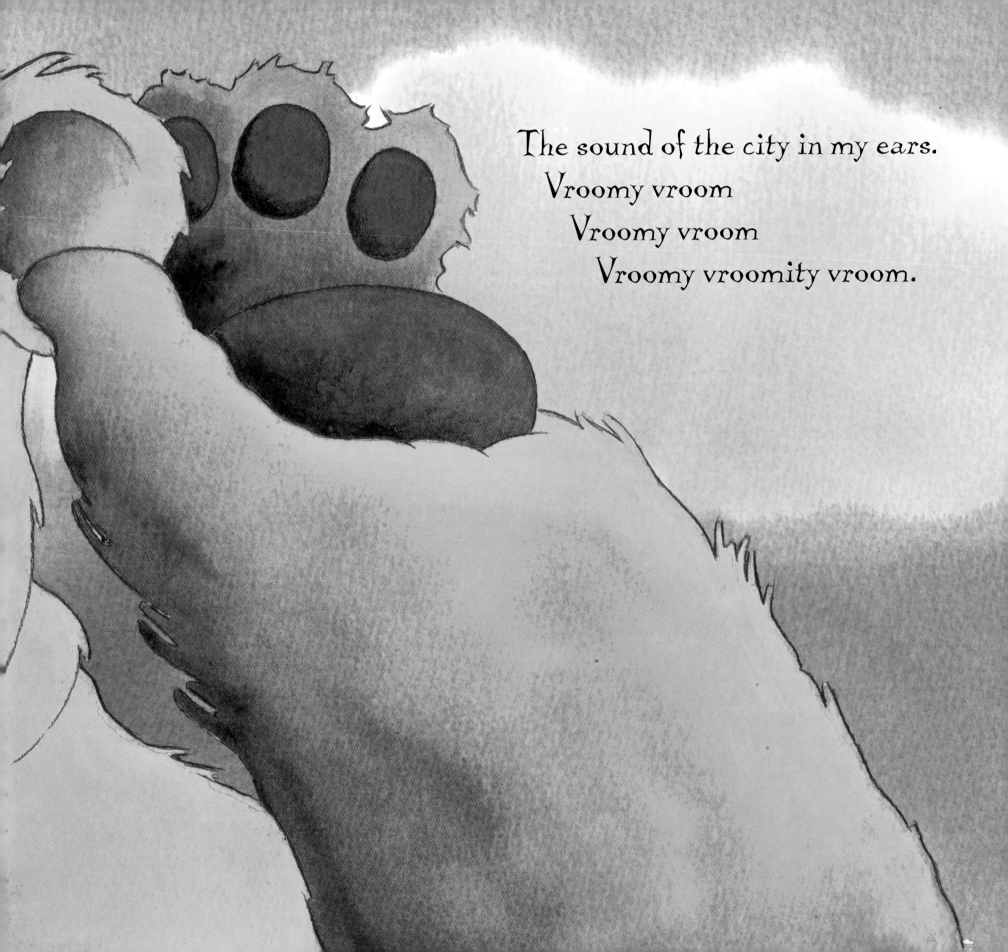

The sound of the city in my ears.
Vroomy vroom
Vroomy vroom
Vroomy vroomity vroom.

So I got a ticket to the city.
To the city?
To the city.

And I travelled to the city far away.
Chuffity chuff
Chuffity chuff
Chuff chuffity chuff.

I saw buildings up to the sky.
Up to the sky?
Up to the sky.

I saw people rushing past.
Rushing past?
Rushing past.

And cars flew by all day.
Whooshy whoosh
Whooshy whoosh
Whooshy whooshity whoosh.

I went to the market.
To the market?
To the market.

I ran to the park.
To the park?
To the park.

I sat on a swing.
On a swing?
On a swing.

But everyone laughed at me there.
Hee hee hee
Hee hee hee
Hee hee heedily hee.

I ran away down the street.
Down the street?
Down the street.

I sat on a bench.
On a bench?
On a bench.

And I heard some people coming near.
They said, 'It's a bear!'
It's a bear?
It's a bear.

'It looks like it's lost.'
Like it's lost?
Like it's lost.

'Let's take it home by the sea.
Follow us
Follow us
Follow ussity us.'

Through the park.
Hee hee hee
Hee hee hee
Hee hee heedily hee.

Through the market.
You gotta buy this
You gotta buy that
You gotta buy thissety this.

Past the cars.
Whooshy whoosh
Whooshy whoosh
Whooshy whooshity whoosh.

On the train.
Chuffity chuff
Chuffity chuff
Chuff chuffity chuff.

The city in my ears.
Vroomy vroom
Vroomy vroom
Vroomy vroomity vroom.

To play by the waves.
Splishety splash
Splishety splash
Splishety splashety splish.

To sing all day.

Do bee doo, do bee doo,

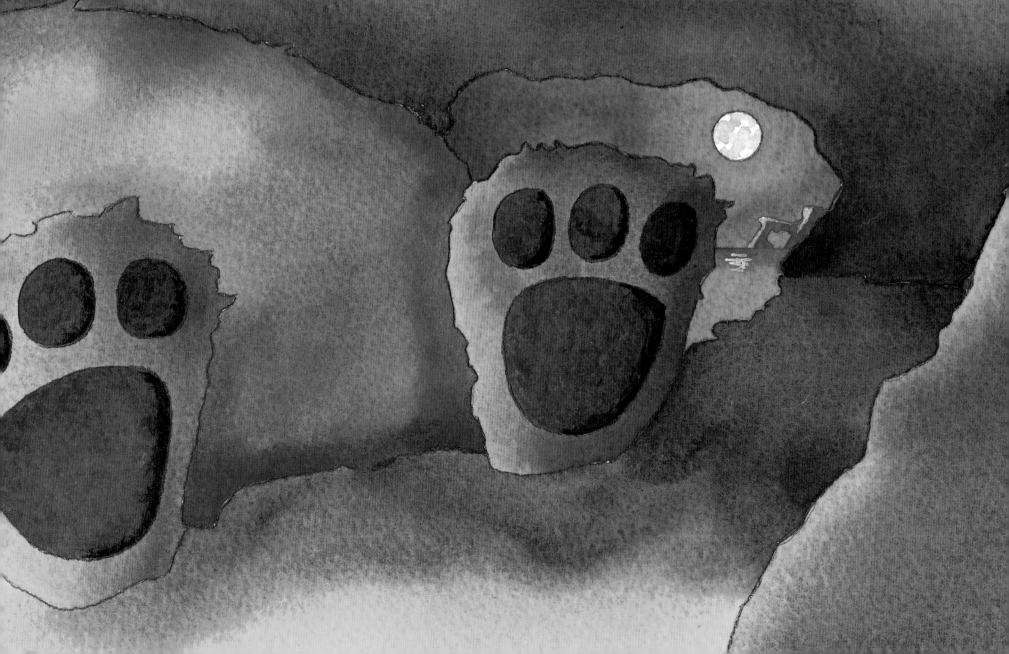

do bee doodily . . . shh.